Half and Half

by

James Sherman

SAMUEL FRENCH

FOUNDED 1830

NEW YORK HOLLYWOOD LONDON TORONTO

SAMUELFRENCH.COM

ISBN 978-0-573-66243-0   Printed in U.S.A.   #10184

IMPORTANT BILLING AND CREDIT REQUIREMENTS

HALF AND HALF received its world premiere at the Victory Gardens Theater (Dennis Zacek, Artistic Director) in Chicago, IL on May 26, 2006. The director was Dennis Zacek. The set design was by Mary Griswold. The lighting design was by Rita Pietraszek. The costume design was by Christine Pascual. The sound design was by Andre Pluess. The production stage manager was Tina M. Jach. The cast was as follows:

SUSAN/LUCY(Act Two)............................ Laura T. Fisher

STEWART/JEREMY.................................Joe Dempsey

LUCY(Act One)/**KATIE**.........................Mattie Hawkinson

HALF AND HALF was subsequently presented by the Penguin Repertory Company (Joe Brancato, Artistic Director and Andrew M. Horn, Executive Director) in Stony Point, NY on May 18, 2007. The director was Joe Brancato. The set design was by Ken Larson. The lighting design was by Peter F. Petrino. The costume design was by Cheryl A. McCarron. The sound design was by Mark Goodloe. The production stage manager was Rosie Goldman. The cast was as follows:

SUSAN/LUCY(Act Two)......................... Dee Dee Friedman

STEWART/JEREMY................................ Sam Guncler

LUCY(Act One)/**KATIE**............................. Leah Karpel

CHARACTERS

ACT ONE

SUSAN
STEWART – Her husband.
LUCY – Their fifteen year old daughter.

PLACE
The kitchen of their home in the Rogers Park area of Chicago.

TIME
April 22, 1970

ACT TWO

LUCY
JEREMY – Her husband.
KATIE – Their fifteen year old daughter.

PLACE
The kitchen of their home in the Rogers Park area of Chicago.

TIME
July 5, 2005

NOTE: One actress plays Susan and Lucy(Act Two). One actor plays Stewart and Jeremy. One actress plays Lucy (Act One) and Katie.

ACT 1

EARTH DAY

*(**AT RISE:** It's April 22, 1970.* SUSAN *is making orange juice with an old fashioned glass juice squeezer.* STEW-ART *is sitting at the table with a cup of coffee while he is reading the newspaper.* SUSAN *has sliced a number of oranges in half. One by one, she takes a half of an orange and manually squeezes the juice into the squeezer. With strength and determination, she squeezes as much juice as she can out of each orange. When each orange has been squeezed out, she drops it into the trash can and picks up the next one. Eventually,* SUSAN *has squeezed enough oranges. She opens a cabinet and gets a glass. She opens a drawer and gets a strainer and puts the strainer over the top of the glass. She picks up the juice squeezer and pours the juice from the squeezer through the strainer into the glass, puts down the juice squeezer, shakes the strainer so that as much juice as possible goes into the glass, removes the strainer, takes the strainer to the trash can, shakes the pulp out of the strainer into the trash, takes the strainer to the sink, rinses it out, puts it in the dish drain, picks up the glass of juice, takes the glass to the table, and puts it down in front of* STEWART.*)*

SUSAN. Here's your juice.

(Silently, STEWART *picks up the glass of juice and takes a drink.* SUSAN *goes back to the counter. She rinses the juice squeezer in the sink and puts it in the dish drain. She washes her hands. She goes to the refrigerator and opens it. She gathers up a loaf of bread, a bowl that is covered with Saran Wrap [there is chicken salad in the*

7

bowl], and a head of lettuce. She puts all three things on the counter. She opens the package of bread and removes two slices and closes the package. She proceeds to make a sandwich. **LUCY** *enters.)*

LUCY. *(sleepily)* Hi.

SUSAN. Good morning. Your juice is on the table.

*(***LUCY*** *goes to her glass of juice and drinks it.)*

SUSAN. *(continuing)* Did you finish your homework?

LUCY. Yes.

SUSAN. All of it?

LUCY. Yes.

SUSAN. Completely?

LUCY. Yes.

*(***LUCY*** *takes another drink.)*

LUCY. *(continuing)* I just have one paper to do.

SUSAN. Lucy…

LUCY. It won't take long.

SUSAN. Well, go do it.

*(***LUCY*** *finishes her drink and heads off.)*

LUCY. *(referring to* **STEWART***)* Is he talking yet?

SUSAN. Nope.

LUCY. Bummer.

*(***LUCY*** *exits. Susan goes to a drawer, opens it, and takes out a plastic sandwich bag and a small paper bag. She puts the sandwich into the sandwich bag, puts the bag into the paper bag, and folds over the top to seal it. She places the bag on the counter where* **STEWART** *will pick it up on his way out.)*

SUSAN. Here's your lunch.

*(***SUSAN*** *goes back to the refrigerator and removes a covered casserole.)*

Stewart.

(He doesn't respond.)

Stewart.

(He looks up at her.)

This is your dinner. It's all ready. I should be home by eight, but I know you don't like to wait so I made this for you.

(He goes back to his newspaper.)

SUSAN. *(continuing)* All you have to do –

(She sees that he isn't paying attention.)

Stewart. Please. I'm trying to make this as easy as I can. I can deal with the Silent Treatment, but I need you to listen.

(He looks up at her.)

All you have to do is preheat the oven at three hundred and fifty degrees, put the casserole in for thirty minutes, and it'll be all ready. All right?

*(He goes back to his newspaper. **SUSAN** returns the casserole to the refrigerator. She closes the refrigerator door and refers to a slip of paper that is attached to the door by a magnet.)*

I wrote it down for you. It's right here. I'll probably be home by eight. Nine at the latest. Of course, if I get arrested, it'll be later. But don't wait up. If I get arrested, I'll call David to come bail me out.

STEWART. No…I don't think that's a good idea.

SUSAN. Why not?

*(**SUSAN** takes a pen out of his shirt pocket and makes figures in the margin of the newspaper.)*

STEWART. Legal fees for David are fifty dollars an hour. Plus extra cause it's after hours. Plus travel. It could cost a hundred, a hundred and fifty dollars.

SUSAN. So that's what's bothering you? If I go to the demonstration, it might cost you some money?

(Pause.)

If I get arrested, will you come and bail me out?

(He looks up and considers it.)

You'd rather I just stayed in jail.

STEWART. I think you're hoping to get arrested.

SUSAN. No, I'm not hoping to get arrested. I just don't know what's going to happen. Nobody's ever done anything like this before. They say there's going to be a lot of people in the plaza. And with the Chicago police, you know, you never know. It could be sixty-eight all over again. If I get arrested, I'll call Mary Anne, all right? I certainly don't want you to do anything that might embarrass you.

STEWART. I'm not embarrassed. I just don't understand why you're not embarrassed.

SUSAN. Why should I be embarrassed about caring about the Earth's environment?

STEWART. What business is it of yours?

SUSAN. You're not concerned about air pollution? Water pollution? The whole point of Earth Day –

STEWART. I'm only concerned about things that I can see.

SUSAN. Well, stay tuned. Pretty soon you may be able to see the air you breathe.

*(**LUCY** enters, carrying a gas mask.)*

LUCY. What is this?

SUSAN. That? Oh, that's uh…That's a gas mask.

*(**STEWART** looks up from his newspaper.)*

LUCY. *(to **SUSAN**)* Are you going to get gassed? You think they're going to throw tear gas at you?

SUSAN. No. No. I don't think so. No. We want to make people aware of the damage that is being done to the environment. We're going to march downtown wearing gas masks to demonstrate what life might be like fifty years from now if we don't start taking care of the earth's environment.

LUCY. Can you breathe with that thing on?

SUSAN. Yes, of course. I think so. I haven't tried it on yet.

(She puts the gas mask on over her head. But she's never put on a gas mask before and she gets struggles with the straps. STEWART sees her.)

STEWART. Oh, for Pete's sake.

(He gets up and goes over to SUSAN. He deftly fixes the gas mask on her.)

If you're going to wear this, wear it correctly.

(He fastens the straps so that the mask is on SUSAN nice and tight.)

LUCY. Where did you learn how to put on a gas mask?

STEWART. I had to wear one once.

(But that's all he has to say on the subject. He goes back to the table and picks up his newspaper.)

LUCY. *(to SUSAN)* Can you breathe?

SUSAN. Yes, fine.

LUCY. Can I try it?

STEWART. No.

LUCY. *(appealing to SUSAN)* Mom?

STEWART. *(more sternly)* No.

LUCY. I just want to –

STEWART. No.

(LUCY gives up.)

LUCY. You're so uptight. Man.

SUSAN. Lucy.

LUCY. What?

SUSAN. Go finish your homework.

(LUCY exits. SSTEWART takes a drink of his coffee which is low in the cup.)

(through the gas mask) Do you want more coffee?

(She goes to the coffee pot, picks it up, takes it to the table, and refills STEWART's coffee cup.)

STEWART. *(referring to the gas mask)* Would you take that off?

(SUSAN returns the coffee pot and removes the gas mask.)

SUSAN. If we don't start to take action against air pollution, water pollution…We are killing the earth. We will leave a dead planet for our children.

(The telephone rings. STEWART puts down his newspaper and goes to answer the phone. While STEWART talks on the phone, SUSAN gets a frying pan ready to fry the eggs.)

STEWART. *(into phone)* Hello?…Good morning, Mother… Yes, Mother…Yes, Mother. We were just discussing that.

SUSAN. No we weren't.

STEWART. *(continuing into phone)* That's not yet been resolved.

SUSAN. Oh, yes it has.

STEWART. *(continuing into phone)* No, Mother…Yes, Mother. I have…Yes, Mother. She's right here.

(He holds out the phone to SUSAN.)

It's your mother.

(SUSAN frantically motions that she doesn't want to take the phone.)

STEWART. She knows you're here.

(SUSAN continues to motion.)

Talk to her.

(SUSAN mouths "No.")

(insistent) Talk to her.

(More insistently, SUSAN mouths "No.")

(more insistently) It's your mother.

(SUSAN stops, accepts the inevitable, and takes the phone. At that moment, LUCY enters. SUSAN holds out the phone to LUCY.)

SUSAN. *(to* LUCY*)* Talk to your grandma.

*(*LUCY *mouths "No." * SUSAN *holds the phone out to her. Accepting the inevitable, * LUCY *takes the phone.)*

LUCY. *(into phone)* Hi, Grandma...It's Lucy...Fine, thank you...Fine...Regular stuff. Math. Science. English...I don't know...No, Grandma, I haven't started thinking about college yet. I don't know if I'm going to go to college.

SUSAN. You're going to college.

*(While * LUCY *is talking on the phone, * SUSAN *takes two eggs out of the carton and returns the carton to the refrigerator. She cracks the two eggs into the frying pan and fries them up.)*

LUCY. *(continuing into phone)* I don't know. I'm not really thinking about the future. I'm just being in the moment. You know. Be here now...Here...Where is here? Here is wherever I am now. Everybody should just be here now...No. I'm not saying you should be here now. You should be wherever you are now. You be there and I'll be – Grandma, I got to go to school, okay?...Okay. Bye. Hold on.

*(*LUCY *hands the phone back to * SUSAN *and gets herself cereal, milk, a bowl, and a spoon and sits at the table to eat.)*

SUSAN. *(to* LUCY*)* You are going to college.

(into phone)

Hello...Yes, Mother...Yes, I am...Because I think it's important...Yes. Today, it's more important than taking care of my husband...Well, actually, I'm not ashamed of myself. And I wish you weren't ashamed of me...I don't care if someone who knows me sees me. I want people to see me. I want people to know I'm one of the people who cares about the environment. Although it'll be difficult to recognize me. I'll be wearing a gas mask...To symbolize the fact that toxic fumes from cars and trucks are polluting the air we breathe. Didn't you read the material I left you?...

(reciting)

Today has been declared Earth Day. Senator Gaylord Nelson of Wisconsin came up with the idea of using the same approach as anti-war teach-ins to raise people's consciousness about the environment. A hundred and forty three million tons of pollution are released into the air of this country every year by cars and trucks, power plants, garbage incinerators –

(stopping the recitation)

Mother...Mother, stop crying. There's no reason for you to...I don't know what's happening to me either, but I don't think you have to cry about it...Mother, do you think you can stop crying?...Mother, if you don't stop crying, I'm going to hang up on you...Mother?... Will you stop crying?...Mother, I'm going to hang up the phone...Mother?!...Mother?!!...Ugh!

(She slams down the phone.)

STEWART. *(incredulous)* You hung up on your mother.

LUCY. Far out.

SUSAN. *(finding it hard to believe herself)* I hung up on my mother.

(She lets the feeling overtake her.)

That feels great.

STEWART. You've never hung up on your mother.

SUSAN. From now on, if she cries, I'm hanging up. I don't need that.

STEWART. I can't believe it.

(SUSAN gets a plate and a spatula and transfers the eggs to the plate.)

SUSAN. What can't you believe, Stewart? That I might have an independent thought separate from you or my mother? That I might not always do just what I'm expected to do?

(*putting the plate in front of* **STEWART**)

Here're your eggs.

(**STEWART** *looks down at the eggs.*)

STEWART. (*observing*) The yolks are broken.

(*Instantly,* **SUSAN** *takes the plate back.*)

SUSAN. Oh, I'm terribly sorry.

STEWART. No, that's –

SUSAN. I'll just make you some more.

STEWART. It's all right.

SUSAN. No. I know you don't like your eggs when the yolks are broken.

(*to* **LUCY**)

You want some eggs?

LUCY. Yuck. No. The yolks are broken.

(**SUSAN** *takes the eggs to the trash can.*)

STEWART. You don't have to –

(**SUSAN** *plops the eggs into the trash.*)

SUSAN. I don't want you thinking I'm falling down on the job around here. I'll just make you some more eggs.

(*The telephone rings.* **STEWART** *gets up to answer it.*)

STEWART. I bet that's her again.

SUSAN. If she cries, I hang up.

STEWART. (*into phone*) Hello?...Yes, one moment.

(*to* **LUCY**)

It's for you.

(**LUCY** *gets up from the table.*)

LUCY. I'll take it in the den.

(**LUCY** *exits.*)

LUCY. (*continuing; as she goes*) Can I get my own phone?

STEWART. No.

(*He listens and then hangs up the phone.*)

STEWART. I can't believe you hung up on your mother.

SUSAN. Who's side are you on?

STEWART. I'm not on anybody's side.

SUSAN. Well, do you think you could be on my side today? Do you think – sometimes – you could be on my side? Sometimes, I'd like to feel your support.

STEWART. Who bought you the new vacuum cleaner?

SUSAN. You're a good provider. That's different.

STEWART. That's a top of the line piece of equipment. That's the most advanced, dependable item on the market today. Comes with all the latest conveniences. That piece of equipment will run for years and never give you a problem.

SUSAN. Are you talking about the vacuum cleaner or me?

(LUCY enters.)

LUCY. That was Hilary Green. She said she can't come to my party.

SUSAN. Why not?

LUCY. She said her mother told her she doesn't want her to be exposed to my hippie mother.

SUSAN. *(incredulous)* What?

LUCY. Like my Sweet Sixteen is going to be some free love sex orgy.

SUSAN. Well, that's just…Did you tell her there aren't going to be any boys there?

LUCY. Yes. And she said her mother said you're a women's libber and all women's libbers hate men and they all become lesbians.

STEWART. That's what I've heard.

SUSAN. *(to LUCY)* Do you want me to call her mother?

LUCY. I tried that. She said her mother wouldn't talk to you. She said her mother thinks you're crazy.

SUSAN. Well, I am not crazy.

LUCY. She said her mother said you don't even know your own name.

SUSAN. What?

(realizing the inference)

Oh, not that again.

LUCY. *(not getting it)* What?

SUSAN. That time we went to the dinner for Daddy's company. When you arrive, there are name tags. I took a name tag and wrote my name on it. Susan Grant. Bud and Barbara Green were there talking to some people so we go over and say hello. Bud Green introduces us to the other couple and says, "This is Stew Grant. This is Stew Grant's wife." I said, "I'm Susan Grant." Well, I guess he thought this was amusing for some reason like I was making a joke. He looks at me as if I've said something incorrect and he says, "You're Stew Grant's wife. I said, "No. I'm Susan Grant." Again, he corrects me. "You're Stew Grant's wife." I pointed to my name tag and said, "No. I'm Susan Grant." Five times, we went back and forth like this. The man refused to accept what I was saying.

LUCY. Male chauvinist pig.

SUSAN. Exactly. It was infuriating.

STEWART. What was infuriating was you trying to humiliate someone I work for.

SUSAN. I wasn't trying to humiliate him. He wasn't humiliated. He thought it was a big joke. Why weren't you concerned about me being humiliated by Bud Green?

STEWART. Why weren't you concerned about me being humiliated in front of the whole meeting?

SUSAN. How was I supposed to know he was the keynote speaker?

(to LUCY)

He opened his speech by relating this amusing anecdote that took place earlier in the evening.

LUCY. So everybody heard it. And I bet Hilary will tell everybody at school and no one will come to my party. What's the point of having a teach-in if no one is going to be there to see it?

STEWART. What do you mean "a teach-in?"

(**LUCY** *stops and looks at* **SUSAN**.)

LUCY. Oops.

STEWART. *(repeating)* What do you mean "a teach-in."

SUSAN. *(to* **STEWART***)* We haven't worked out all the details yet.

STEWART. So you're playing "Don't Tell Daddy."

(*to* **LUCY**)

Tell me.

SUSAN. Lucy came up with this brilliant idea.

STEWART. What.

(**LUCY** *looks to* **SUSAN**. **SUSAN** *motions for* **LUCY** *to go ahead.*)

LUCY. *(to* **STEWART***)* I was at Laurie Feldman's Sweet Sixteen and she got a bunch of jewelry and clothes and about a thousand stuffed animals and I thought, "I don't want any of this stuff." So I decided to make my Sweet Sixteen party a teach-in about the objectification of women.

STEWART. *(to* **SUSAN**, *dubious)* And this was Lucy's idea.

LUCY. I'm going to decorate the room with Playboy magazines and I just can't decide if we should dress up like Playboy bunnies or if I should call the Playboy Club and invite some actual bunnies to be there.

STEWART. At the restaurant?

LUCY. Well, I'm thinking if we have actual bunnies there, we have a better chance of getting some media attention.

STEWART. Great.

(*to* **SUSAN**)

The next thing you know, she'll be on T.V...Sitting in a courtroom strapped to a chair like Bobby Seale!

SUSAN. *(to* **LUCY***)* Go get your things together for school.

(**LUCY** *exits.*)

STEWART. Well, now you've ruined her party.

SUSAN. I've ruined her party?

STEWART. And I bet this means you can forget about the couples club.

SUSAN. The couples club? Fine. Who cares?

STEWART. I do.

SUSAN. Because you get to sit with the men and play poker. I'm stuck in the kitchen with the wives playing Mah Jongg.

STEWART. You like Mah Jongg.

SUSAN. I hate Mah Jongg.

STEWART. You hate Mah Jongg?

SUSAN. Last time we were there, I said why don't we play poker and let the men play Mah Jongg?

STEWART. Don't be silly.

SUSAN. Why is that silly?

STEWART. Women don't play poker.

SUSAN. Women don't play poker? What, is there a poker gene that we lack? Does having ovaries somehow make us biologically incapable of playing poker? Is there some natural selection so we have opposable thumbs to carry the children and clean the house but we can't hold playing cards?

STEWART. I can't imagine Barbara Green playing poker.

SUSAN. Because Barbara Green is a nincompoop. It's impossible to have an intelligent conversation with her.

STEWART. You're not there to have an intelligent conversation.

SUSAN. Obviously not. There are things going on in the world. The environment. Viet Nam. Nixon. Those women absolutely refuse…

STEWART. They're there to play Mah Jongg.

SUSAN. So we can't talk about what's going on in the world?

STEWART. They don't want to hear what you have to say.

SUSAN. No, you don't want to hear what I have to say. Why can't you be on my side, Stewart? Sometimes. I would like to feel that you're on my side. Could you do that? Could you say, "Susan. I'm on your side. When times get rough. And friends just can't be found. Like a bridge over troubled water." Will you lay yourself down?

STEWART. I have no idea what you're talking about.

(laying down the law)

If we are invited to the couples club, you will go and you will behave yourself. Lucy will have her Sweet Sixteen party at the Kon Tiki Ports as planned and on your name tag it will say Mrs. Stewart Grant and there will be no more discussion about it.

SUSAN. No, there will be more discussion about it.

(beginning a new conversation)

Stewart. We have to talk.

STEWART. I am not going to call you Susan Grant.

SUSAN. Why not? It's my name. Do you know who I am?

STEWART. Yes, I know who you are. You are my wife. You are the mother of my daughter.

SUSAN. That's not enough.

STEWART. It was enough for my mother.

SUSAN. How do you know?

STEWART. She never complained that being a wife and a mother wasn't enough.

SUSAN. How do you know she didn't complain?

STEWART. My parents never argued.

SUSAN. Of course they never argued. They barely talked to each other. Your father got up, had one piece of toast and one soft boiled egg, went to work for ten hours, came home, they ate dinner in silence, and he went to bed. Just because she didn't complain doesn't mean she wasn't unhappy.

STEWART. So what are you saying? You're unhappy?

SUSAN. Yes, Stewart. I am unhappy.

(LUCY *enters, carrying a book, a pen, and a notebook.*)

SUSAN. Did you do your paper?

LUCY. I'm doing it.

SUSAN. Lucy…

LUCY. Can you just help me?

SUSAN. What's it about?

LUCY. "The Road Not Taken" by Robert Frost. I don't get it.

SUSAN. What don't you get?

LUCY. Well, two roads diverged in a yellow wood, right?

SUSAN. Yes.

LUCY. There's, like, a fork in the road, right? So he has to decide which road to take.

SUSAN. So what's the problem?

LUCY. I don't get it when he says, "I took the one less traveled by and that has made all the difference." What's the difference?

SUSAN. He took the road less traveled by.

LUCY. But, before, he says…Wait.

(*She opens her book and reads.*)

(*reading*) "Though as for that the passing there had worn them really about the same." So what's the difference?

SUSAN. Let me see.

(LUCY *hands the book to* SUSAN.)

SUSAN. (*reads*) "Two roads diverged in a yellow wood."

(*skimming ahead*)

Da-da-da-da-da.

(*reads*)

"Then took the other as just as fair, and having perhaps the better claim."

(*continuing, with emphasis*)

"Because it was grassy and wanted wear."

(to **LUCY***)*

So they weren't the same.

LUCY. But, no, see, he says, "Though as for that the passing there had worn them really about the same. And both that morning equally lay in leaves no step had trodden black."

SUSAN. All right. So they look the same. But he still has to make a decision.

(reads)

"Oh, I kept the first for another day. Yet knowing how way leads on to way, I doubted if I would ever come back." So you have to choose.

LUCY. And once you make a choice, you can never go back to where you were.

STEWART. You make choices. You don't know what's going to happen.

LUCY. So even if you don't know what lies ahead –

SUSAN. Especially if you don't know what lies ahead.

LUCY. Sometimes you have to be brave.

SUSAN. If you're going to take the road less traveled by, you have to be brave, yes. You can follow the crowd like most people or you can be a leader. Take the road less traveled by. And make a difference.

LUCY. Groovy.

SUSAN. You know what you could do? You could go to school today – Follow the crowd like most people – Or…You could choose to go with me to Earth Day.

LUCY. I could?

SUSAN. You could.

LUCY. *(happily)* Far out.

*(***SUSAN*** holds out her hand palm-up.)*

SUSAN. Slip me some skin, Sister.

LUCY. Yeah!

(**LUCY** *slides her hand down* **SUSAN***'s hand.*)

SUSAN. You're my sister.

STEWART. She's your daughter.

SUSAN. She's my sister.

STEWART. She's your daughter. And she's not going out on the street with a bunch of hippies and bra burners.

SUSAN. Nobody is burning bras.

STEWART. I read it in the paper. The hippies are burning their draft cards. The women's libbers are burning bras.

SUSAN. Nobody's burning bras. There was one demonstration in Atlantic City to protest the Miss America pageant and some bras and girdles were tossed into the Freedom Trash Can as a symbol to liberate women from those awful, constricting undergarments.

STEWART. They're not so constricting.

SUSAN. How often do you wear a bra and girdle?

LUCY. *(laughing)* I'd like to see Daddy in a bra and girdle.

STEWART. Women have been wearing them for a long time. There's nothing wrong with them.

SUSAN. I'm not wearing a bra and I can't tell you how good it feels.

STEWART. You're not wearing a bra?

LUCY. Neither am I.

STEWART. *(flabbergasted)* What? You –

(*He turns to* **LUCY** *and then realizes he must turn away and cover his eyes.*)

You are not leaving this house with your…Things flopping around.

LUCY. I do it all the time.

SUSAN. There's nothing wrong with it.

STEWART. *(towards* **LUCY***)* You go right upstairs and put a bra on, Little Miss. Or you will be grounded forever.

LUCY. *(appealing to* **SUSAN***)* Mom…

STEWART. I mean it!

(After a beat, SUSAN *acquiesces.)*

SUSAN. *(to* LUCY*)* Go on.

LUCY. *(whining)* Ohhhh...

*(*LUCY *storms out.)*

STEWART. You're putting these ideas in her head.

SUSAN. I'm not putting ideas in her head. She's a smart girl. She knows what's going on in the world.

STEWART. How is she going to get into college if she has an arrest record along with her transcripts?

SUSAN. Maybe there are more important things than college.

STEWART. Do not put that idea in her head.

SUSAN. I'm not worried about Lucy. Lucy is a leader. She will accomplish whatever she wants to do. Maybe the most important thing is for her to have someone who will support her in what she wants to do. Can we get back to what I was saying?

STEWART. What were you saying?

SUSAN. I was saying I am unhappy. Do you remember that?

STEWART. Yes.

SUSAN. Stewart. I think we should see a marriage counselor.

STEWART. I don't need to see a marriage counselor.

SUSAN. There's nothing wrong with it. I think we have some problems in our marriage and there are people who –

STEWART. I don't have any problems in our marriage.

SUSAN. Yes, you do.

STEWART. No, I don't.

SUSAN. Yes, you do. If I have a problem in our marriage then we have to work on the problem together.

STEWART. If you have a problem, that's your problem.

SUSAN. You don't think you have a problem?

STEWART. I don't have a problem.

SUSAN. If I say I have a problem in our marriage, you don't

think, then, that you have a problem?

STEWART. I don't have a problem.

SUSAN. You don't think that if I have a problem in our marriage that, as my husband, it would be to your benefit to help me fix my problem? Will you do that?

STEWART. No.

SUSAN. *(yells)* That's the problem!

STEWART. Keep your voice down.

SUSAN. I have been keeping my voice down for eighteen years. I can not keep my voice down any longer.

STEWART. Calm down or I will not have this conversation.

SUSAN. *(calming down)* All right. All right.

(trying a new approach)

All right. Look. I know you're not going to be happy about this, but I have something to tell you.

(He waits for it.)

SUSAN. I've been going to a women's consciousness raising group.

(He continues to listen.)

SUSAN. Lately, when I've been saying I'm going to the movies with Mary Ann, I've been going to this group. We meet at the Y down in the Loop and, I don't know how to describe it…It's amazing. These women come together in a room and we're not anyone's wife, we're not anyone's mother, we're just…People.

*(**STEWART** is staring off in another direction.)*

Are you listening?

*(**STEWART** looks at her.)*

STEWART. Hm? Yes, I'm listening. You've been going to a consciousness raising group.

SUSAN. Yes.

STEWART. Hmm. I thought you were having an affair.

SUSAN. *(astonished)* What?

STEWART. When you said you went to see "Funny Girl" with Mary Ann. When you came home, you didn't say anything about the movie. You didn't sing any of the songs.

SUSAN. You don't like musicals.

STEWART. That never stopped you before. So the next time you said you were going to a movie, I checked the odometer in the car.

SUSAN. You what?

STEWART. Before you went and after you came back. You drove eight point two miles. You said you had gone to the Granada Theatre. So, the next day, I drove to the Granada Theatre and from here to the Granada Theatre is only one point four miles. So even if you had gone to the Granada Theatre, obviously, you had also gone someplace else.

SUSAN. So you assumed I was having an affair? Why didn't you ask me?

STEWART. I assumed if you were having an affair, I assumed you'd lie about it.

SUSAN. I'm not having an affair.

STEWART. I'm glad to hear it. But you did lie about going to the movies.

SUSAN. Yes, I did. I'm sorry.

STEWART. So you've been going to consciousness raising groups.

SUSAN. Yes. I didn't know what you'd think –

STEWART. Well, I'll tell you what I think.

SUSAN. What?

STEWART. I think it's nonsense.

SUSAN. It's not nonsense, Stewart. If you'd think about it... If you'd be willing to think about it...If you'd be willing to talk about it with me, you'd see that it makes a lot of sense. I have a problem.

STEWART. What's the problem?

SUSAN. It's the problem that has no name.

STEWART. Wait. You have a problem but you can't tell me what it is?

SUSAN. No, I'm telling you what it is. Women today are dealing with the problem that has no name.

STEWART. It doesn't have a name.

SUSAN. That's right.

STEWART. Then it can't be much of a problem.

SUSAN. It is, Stewart. It's a very big problem.

STEWART. It can't be a very big problem if it doesn't have a name. Everything has a name. This is a table. This is a cup. This is a plate. And I'd like to have some eggs on it.

SUSAN. *(retreating)* Fine.

STEWART. Can you give your problem a name? If you give it a name, you can tell me what it is, and I'll fix it.

SUSAN. This isn't a problem like there's a leaky faucet or the car won't start. It's a feeling. I've had it for a long time. And I didn't know what to call it. What name to give it. But I couldn't make it go away.

(confessing)

Sometimes, when you're at work and Lucy is at school, I get in the car and drive away.

STEWART. To where?

SUSAN. Anywhere. Away from here. Just to get away for an hour or two. Once, I drove west and suddenly I realized I'd driven all the way to the Mississippi River. I wondered what it would be like to be like Huck Finn and sail down the Mississippi on a raft.

STEWART. Don't be silly.

SUSAN. Why is that silly? This is America, isn't it? The land of the free and the home of the brave. If I want to sail down the Mississippi on a raft, why shouldn't I?

STEWART. Because you're not a child. Because you have responsibilities.

SUSAN. That's right. I stood there and I said, "I can't sail down the Mississippi on a raft. I have to go home and make dinner.

STEWART. Everybody does what they have to do.

SUSAN. But after everybody does what they have to do. After I've made you your breakfast and your lunch and your dinner. After I've washed the dishes and cleaned the house and folded the laundry and shopped for the groceries, there's still this feeling. What's missing?

STEWART. What?

SUSAN. Me! Where am I? I know where the plates are. And the glasses and the forks and the spoons. But what about me? I don't know where I am.

(beat)

But you know what I found out? I found out I'm not the only woman who feels this way. Mary Ann took me to this meeting.

STEWART. At the Y in the Loop.

SUSAN. No, this was before that. Last month. Out at the O'Hare Inn. It was the annual conference of the National Organization for Women.

STEWART. That was the first "movie night?"

SUSAN. I didn't think you'd approve.

STEWART. I don't.

SUSAN. You believe in civil rights for black people, don't you?

STEWART. Of course.

SUSAN. So why shouldn't women have equal rights?

STEWART. What rights don't you have?

SUSAN. Lots of them. That's what I found out at this meeting. I walked in. I can't remember the last time I walked into a room and nobody knew me. I wasn't Stew's wife or Lucy's mom. I was just...Whoever I happen to be. There must have been 200 people crammed into this little conference room. I had to stand up on a chair to see who was speaking. A few people spoke and then, this little woman came up to the front. Betty Friedan, herself, was there. She spoke about equal rights for women. And equal pay for equal work. And equal

opportunities for women in education. And the need
for federally funded day care for women with children
who want to work outside of the home. The woman
has such energy. She spoke for almost two hours. And
then, at the end, she announced that, this summer,
women all over the country are going to go on strike
to show how important women are to society. So I'm
telling you now. August twenty-sixth. You're making
your own dinner.

STEWART. You're going to go on strike?

SUSAN. Yep.

STEWART. How can you go on strike? You don't have a job.

SUSAN. I don't have a job? You don't consider what I do
around here work? That's exactly –

STEWART. Yes, it's work.

SUSAN. Okay then.

STEWART. But you can't call it a job because you don't get
paid for it.

SUSAN. Well, then, maybe I should.

STEWART. Don't be ridiculous.

SUSAN. Why is that ridiculous?

STEWART. I give you everything you need.

SUSAN. No, you give me everything you need. If I wasn't
here, you'd have to pay someone to cook your meals
and wash your clothes. When I go to New York this
summer for the strike, maybe you won't take me for
granted anymore.

STEWART. You're going to New York.

SUSAN. August twenty-sixth.

STEWART. How are you going to get there? I'm not going
to pay for it.

SUSAN. Then I'll pay for it myself.

STEWART. With what?

SUSAN. I'll get my own money. I'm going to get a job.

STEWART. You are not.

SUSAN. Why not?

STEWART. My wife is not going to get a job. What do you think people would say?

SUSAN. *(shrugging)* I don't know.

(getting an idea)

Maybe they'd say, "Look at that lucky so-and-so. His wife is bringing in as much money as he is. They must be rolling in dough."

STEWART. No one is going to hire you. You don't have any skills.

SUSAN. I certainly do have skills. I did go to college.

STEWART. With a major in Home Ec. and a minor in Philosophy. What are you going to do with that?

SUSAN. I have plenty of skills. I run this household. I haven't heard any complaints.

STEWART. *(coming up with a complaint)* My coffee cup is empty.

*(**SUSAN** looks at him and then decides her next move. She gets up, goes to the stove, picks up the coffee pot, and walks over to **STEWART**. But she doesn't pour the coffee. She holds out her hand.)*

SUSAN. That'll be fifty cents.

STEWART. What?

SUSAN. You want more coffee? It'll cost you fifty cents. If you were in a restaurant, you'd pay someone to bring you your coffee.

STEWART. I'm not in a restaurant.

SUSAN. Then get your own coffee.

(She takes the coffee pot back to the stove and then goes and sits down at the table.)

If fact, I'm not waiting until August twenty-sixth. I'm going on strike right now.

STEWART. Get me my coffee. And make me my eggs.

SUSAN. Nope. Make your own damn eggs.

(**STEWART** *gets up.*)

STEWART. I don't know what's gotten into you but I don't like it.

(*He goes to the refrigerator and opens it.*)

What kind of an example are you setting for Lucy?

SUSAN. I think a good one.

(**STEWART** *is standing in front of the open refrigerator. He's looking for the eggs.*)

STEWART. I want you to stay at home. I want you to stop going to those meetings, stop talking about...all those other women. And we can get back to normal around here.

(*He can't find the eggs.*)

Where're the eggs?

SUSAN. How much is it worth to you?

(**STEWART** *slams the door shut.*)

STEWART. I forbid you to go to this ridiculous demonstration today. I forbid you to go to anymore meetings. You will stay home –

SUSAN. No.

STEWART. You will clean this house.

SUSAN. No.

STEWART. And when I get home at five o'clock, you will have dinner on the table.

SUSAN. No! We can't just keep...I'm going out of my mind here.

(*confessing*)

I went to see a psychiatrist. Yeah. I thought, "Hey, there's nothing wrong with you or with Lucy so it must be me. I must be going crazy so I went to see a psychiatrist. I tried to explain my problem. Why do I feel so unhappy? Why do I feel so...Out of place? So you know what the psychiatrist said? He said he's been seeing a lot of women with this problem lately. He said a lot of women are overly anxious these days. He gave me a prescription for tranquilizers. Well, I never went back to see him. I don't want to take tranquilizers. I don't want to tranquilize my feelings. I want to feel my feelings. But I can't feel what I want to feel and just keep doing what I've been doing. How can I make you understand?

(She gets an idea. She goes to a drawer and pulls it out.)

Wait a minute.

(She pulls the drawer all the way out of the cabinet and puts the drawer on the floor. She reaches back inside the cabinet and pulls out a book. It's a copy of "The Feminine Mystique" by Betty Friedan.)

This is what Betty says.

(reading)

"A woman cannot find her identity through others – her husband, her children. They cannot find it in the dull routine of housework.

(farther down the page, she reads)

"If women do not put forth, finally, that effort to become all that they have it in them to become, they will forfeit their own humanity."

(to STEWART)

I'm dying here.

(She waits for him to respond.)

STEWART. How much did the psychiatrist cost?

(She's about to explode with anger, but she holds on to it. She puts the book back into the cabinet and replaces the drawer. She goes to the refrigerator, opens it, and takes out the carton of eggs. She puts the carton on the counter, removes and egg, and cracks it in the pan.)

SUSAN. Oh, I broke the yolk.

(She takes another egg out of the carton and cracks it

open into the frying pan.)

SUSAN. Oh, I broke another yolk.

(With growing intensity, she takes another egg out of the carton and smashes it into the frying pan.)

STEWART. Stop that.

(But SUSAN doesn't stop. She smashes another egg. Then another. STEWART gets up from his chair and goes to her.)

STEWART. Calm down! Calm down!

SUSAN. Stay away from me! I'm going to go where I'm going to go and nothing you do is going to stop me. You just keep on doing what you're doing. Why not? You've got no complaints. You've got no problems. Life, for you, is perfect. You've got everything.

STEWART. *(blowing his lid)* I've got nothing!

(confessing)

I lost my job.

SUSAN. *(confounded)* What? When?

STEWART. Last week. Wednesday.

SUSAN. What happened?

STEWART. Bud let me go.

SUSAN. Why?

STEWART. He's reorganizing. There's a recession. He didn't really say.

(Pause.)

SUSAN. If I let him call me Mrs. Stewart Grant, will he let you keep your job?

STEWART. I don't think so.

SUSAN. What have you been doing?

STEWART. Usually, I go to the Field Museum. Look at the dinosaurs. I have an interview tomorrow for a new job. I'm not worried. I gave the old man twenty years. I figure I'm good for another twenty years someplace else.

SUSAN. I could look for a job, too.

STEWART. You are not going to get a job.

SUSAN. I could try. I'd be happy to –

STEWART. Who cares if you're happy?

SUSAN. You don't care if I'm happy?

STEWART. All I care about is that I have a paycheck coming in, that I'm working with honest people, and that when I come home at the end of the day, my wife will be here waiting for me.

SUSAN. You would rather...? I could work. And I could bring in extra income. And I could find something to do for myself that would be...For myself. But you would rather I stay home. And cook for you and clean for you and do just the things you want me to do... And be miserable.

*(**STEWART** makes his declaration.)*

STEWART. That's right.

*(After a moment, **SUSAN** makes her choice of how to proceed. Silently, she begins to clear the table. She dumps the plates into the sink. **LUCY** enters, drops her book on the table and holds up her paper.)*

LUCY. I'm finished!

SUSAN. Get your coat.

LUCY. You're driving me to school?

SUSAN. You're not going to school. You're going with me.

STEWART. She's going to school.

SUSAN. She's going with me!

STEWART. *(warning)* You go out that door, don't you bother coming back.

SUSAN. Then I won't come back.

STEWART. You're going to leave me here.

SUSAN. I'm sorry, Stewart, I can't save you. I don't know if I can save myself. But I believe...I really believe if I go out there today and do what I can do and say what I can say...I can do something. Starting today, I can save the earth!

(SUSAN *exits.* LUCY *follows her out.* STEWART *stands for a moment. He paces, not knowing what to do. He goes to the table and picks up his coffee cup and takes it to the sink. He stands for a moment. Suddenly, he smashes his fist through the window above the sink. The entire window pane shatters. He holds his fist in pain.*)

(LUCY *enters.*)

LUCY. I need my Robert Frost.

(LUCY *stops when she sees* STEWART. *She sees the pain on his face. They stand and look at each other.*)

BLACKOUT

END OF ACT ONE

ACT 2

ANNIVERSARY DAY

(*THE SETTING:* Same house. Same kitchen. Thirty-five years later. The appliances are newer. There is a microwave, a cordless phone, and an electric juicer. The window is boarded up.)

(*AT RISE:* It's July 5, 2005. **LUCY**, living in the house she grew up in, is sitting at the kitchen table reading the newspaper. In front of her are open law books, legal pads and an open laptop computer. Her husband, **JEREMY**, is squeezing oranges in the electric juicer. When he has squeezed enough juice into the container, he picks up a glass, pours the juice into the glass, and brings it to **LUCY**.)

JEREMY. Here's your juice.

LUCY. Thank you.

(*He returns to the juicer and cleans it out.*)

JEREMY. So I was going to tell you. I was flipping around last night. I catch the old Dick Van Dyke show. One of my favorite episodes. Rob and Laura Petrie have checked into a fancy hotel. They've decided to have a, uh…second honeymoon. So Laura goes into the bathtub to take a bath and she gets her big toe stuck in the bath spout. So Rob –

(**LUCY**'s cell phone rings. She grabs for it.)

LUCY. (*into phone*) Lucy Grant.

(**JEREMY** stops his story.)

JEREMY. All right.

LUCY. (*into phone*) Hello…Yes…No, I haven't received it

yet...I'm looking at my email right in front of me. I
don't have it...No. I have to be in court at nine and I
have to have that report...Well, A.S.A.P. had better be
really S.

(She hangs up. She types something on her laptop.)

JEREMY. Do you want more coffee?

LUCY. *(without looking up)* Yes. Thank you.

*(He pours her a cup of coffee and then gets one for him-
self. She hits one key on her laptop and sits back and
picks up the newspaper.* **JEREMY** *watches her for a
moment. She looks up at him.)*

JEREMY. Sorry to bother you.

LUCY. What?

JEREMY. You got a minute?

LUCY. Yes. What?

JEREMY. I got you something.

LUCY. You got me something?

*(***JEREMY*** pulls a CD out of his pocket.)*

JEREMY. I made you a mix tape.

LUCY. *(perplexed)* That's nice.

*(***JEREMY*** takes the CD over to a boombox and inserts the
disc.)*

JEREMY. All of your favorite hits of the sixties, seventies,
and one from the eighties. "Don't Worry, Be Happy."
But we start it off with a big hit from 1967. Here're the
Foundations.

*(He pushes "play" on the boombox. We hear "Baby, Now
That I've Found You" by The Foundations.* **JEREMY** *goes
to the refrigerator and opens it. He gathers up milk, eggs,
cheese, zucchini, green onion, and a red pepper and puts
them on the counter.)*

FOUNDATIONS (V.O.)

BABY, NOW THAT I'VE FOUND YOU I CAN'T LET YOU
GO.

I'LL BUILD MY WORLD AROUND YOU.
I NEED YOU SO, BABY, EVEN THOUGH YOU DON'T
NEED ME.
YOU DON'T NEED ME.

JEREMY. *(encouraging* **LUCY** *to sing along)* Everybody.

FOUNDATIONS (V.O.)

BABY, NOW THAT I'VE FOUND YOU I CAN'T LET YOU
GO.
I'LL BUILD MY WORLD AROUND YOU.
I NEED YOU SO, BABY, EVEN THOUGH YOU DON'T
NEED ME.
YOU DON'T NEED ME.

(The house phone rings. **JEREMY** *answers it.)*

JEREMY. Hello?…Good morning, Ron…Yes. She's right here.

(He hands the phone to **LUCY.** *)*

(with solemnity) It's Ron.

(She takes the phone from him. While she's on the phone, **JEREMY** *takes the veggies to the sink and washes them. He takes the zucchini to a cutting board, gets a knife, and, with ease and dexterity, slices the zucchini and puts them in a bowl. He will do the same with the green onions and the red pepper.)*

LUCY. *(into phone)* Hello?…Good morning…

(She motions to **JEREMY** *to turn off the music. He does and then goes back to his food prep.)*

LUCY.	**JEREMY.**
(into phone)	*(calling out)*
Yes, Sir. I'm ready…No. No. I've got everything I need. I'm all set to go… Um, I don't know. I guess I could meet you before we go in.	Katie! Come and get some breakfast.

*(***JEREMY*** waves to her to get her attention.)*

JEREMY. *(sotto voce)* No. No. Please. I'm making breakfast.

LUCY. *(into phone)* I don't think I have anything to ask you. Why don't we just meet there?...Yes, I'm wearing my super suit...And the cape. Yes...No problem. I'll see you there...'Bye.

(She presses the off button and puts the phone down.)

LUCY. *(continuing; referring to Ron)* Asshole.

JEREMY. *(concurring)* What an asshole.

(LUCY checks her laptop.)

LUCY. Nothing.

(She sits back. She checks the newspaper. JEREMY continues slicing and dicing.)

JEREMY. Did I tell you my mom called?

(LUCY looks up from her paper.)

LUCY. I'm sorry. What?

JEREMY. My mom and dad want to take us out to dinner this weekend. I was thinking Sunday.

LUCY. Uh...I don't know.

JEREMY. Katie's got a game Sunday morning and I signed up to do a 10K. So if you could take Katie to her game...That'd be a help.

LUCY. I don't know. Hard to say.

JEREMY. Then, after the game, we could meet up with my parents for dinner.

LUCY. I don't know. *(rhetorically)* What can I tell you?

JEREMY. You can tell me you'll go to dinner with me and my parents on Sunday.

LUCY. I'm in the middle of a trial.

JEREMY. How do you know it's the middle? Maybe it'll be over tomorrow and you're at the end of a trial.

(KATIE enters and heads for the refrigerator.)

Do you want some breakfast?

KATIE. I'm okay.

JEREMY. I'm making my special Red Pepper and Zucchini Frittata.

KATIE. Uh…No, thanks.

JEREMY. I can just make you some eggs.

(KATIE *comes out of the refrigerator with a carton of* *yogurt.*)

KATIE. I'm okay.

JEREMY. You need to eat.

KATIE. I am.

(*She gets a spoon from a drawer, opens the yogurt, and* *starts to eat it.*)

JEREMY. Will you eat at lunch?

KATIE. Yes.

JEREMY. Something with carbs?

KATIE. All right.

(*A cell phone rings.* KATIE *reaches into her pocket and* *removes her cell phone. She looks at the display.*)

KATIE. Who is that?

(*She flips the phone open and talks into it.*)

(*into phone*)

Hello?…Good morning…Oh…Yeah, I guess. Hold on…

(*She holds the phone down and addresses* JEREMY.)

It's Dr. Lee's office.

(LUCY *looks up.*)

(*to* JEREMY) They need to change the appointment.

LUCY. Dr. Who?

(KATIE *and* JEREMY *look at each other.*)

KATIE. Oops.

JEREMY. (*to* LUCY) It's just a…thing. It's nothing.

(*to* KATIE)

Yeah. Whatever.

LUCY. What is this?

KATIE. *(into phone)* Sure. That's fine…Friday? I think so.

    (to **JEREMY***)*

    Can we make it Friday instead?

JEREMY. Friday. Yes. Good. Fine.

KATIE. *(into phone)* Friday at five will be fine…Okay. See you then…Bye.

    (She hangs up her phone and starts to go.)

LUCY. Wait.

    *(***KATIE*** stops.)*

    We're playing "Don't tell Mommy?" I hate that.

    (to **KATIE***)* Tell me.

JEREMY. You know I had my check-up with Dr. Handler and I'm always telling him how I feel guilty cause Katie inherited my allergies and it's affecting her breathing and he suggested we take her to see an ear, nose and throat specialist.

KATIE. An otolaryngologist.

JEREMY. Yeah, an oto…What she said. So I just thought we'd make an appointment to get it checked out.

KATIE. I have a deviated septum.

JEREMY. Well, we're not sure. But Dr. Handler thought it would be worth checking out.

LUCY. You're talking about a nose job.

JEREMY. No.

KATIE. *(simultaneously)* No.

JEREMY. Well, sure. Because, you know, when they do the procedure…As long as they're in there…

LUCY. *(to* **KATIE***)* There's nothing wrong with your nose.

KATIE. I knew you were going to say that.

JEREMY. We know there's nothing wrong with her nose. But if it could be improved upon –

LUCY. She's not getting a nose job.

JEREMY. Well, it's not actually a nose job. The procedure is called a rhinoplasty.

LUCY. A rhinoplasty is a nose job.

JEREMY. Well, I may not have the right term exactly. But it's to help her breathe.

KATIE. For my soccer game.

JEREMY. For her soccer game.

LUCY. Her soccer game is fine.

KATIE. It could be better. Coach Kay says –

LUCY. You're the best player on the team.

KATIE. Now. Yeah. But –

JEREMY. If she wants to have a shot at a Division One school.

LUCY. Who says she has to go to a Division One school?

JEREMY. We talked about it.

LUCY. And we said a Division Three school isn't as high pressure.

JEREMY. But Katie came up with this great idea. If she does get any offers from Division One schools, the Division Three schools will throw the scholarships at her.

KATIE. If I can breathe better.

JEREMY. If she can breathe better.

KATIE. *(to LUCY)* Can I, at least, talk to the doctor about it?

LUCY. No.

KATIE. It doesn't cost anything.

LUCY. No.

KATIE. I just want to see –

LUCY. No.

KATIE. *(vexed)* That is so random!

LUCY. *(to JEREMY)* Why didn't you talk to me about this?

JEREMY. You've barely been home.

KATIE. It's my nose. I can do what I want with it.

LUCY. No, you can't.

KATIE. I thought you were pro-choice.

(**LUCY** *gives her a stern look and points an accusatory finger at her.*)

JEREMY. (*to* **KATIE** Bad move.

(*The telephone rings.* **JEREMY** *goes to answer it.*)

(*into phone*) Hello?...Hello?...Susan! Hi. How're you doing?

(*to* **LUCY**) It's your mom.

(*into phone*) What?...Yes. I can hear you. Where are you?... Really? Wow... Yeah. I'm sure it is... No. No, I've never been there. I'd love to get there sometime... We're all good...What?...Oh, well, thank you. That's nice of you to remember...Well, that's kind of an open question...Yeah, Katie's here. She's good. She's busy with school...I'm all right...No, I haven't been finding the time to do any writing. I have the beginnings of the makings of a seed of an idea. Maybe something'll come of it...Well, we'll see...Are you coming to the States anytime soon?...Oh, yeah. I saw that in the paper. I'm sorry...Oh, yeah? Really? Well, we'll look forward to seeing you...Sure, she's right here.

(**LUCY** *frantically motions that she doesn't want to take the phone.*)

LUCY. (*referring to* **KATIE**) Let her talk to her.

(**JEREMY** *offers the phone to* **KATIE**.)

JEREMY. Talk to your Grandma.

(**KATIE** *takes the phone.*)

LUCY. (*to* **KATIE**, *through clenched teeth*) Do not say anything about getting a nose job.

(*While* **KATIE** *is on the phone,* **JEREMY** *is preparing the eggs and veggies in a skillet on the stove.*)

KATIE. (*into phone*) Hello?...Hi, Grandma. It's Katie. Hi...I'm fine. How are you?...Where are you?... Wow. Cool...I'm just getting ready for school...Yeah. Summer school...Well, I figured it out. If I go to full time summer school, I can be done with high school in three years, then I can do college in three years, and I can be through law school by the time I'm twenty-one…Because then, that gives me a good six to eight years to make partner. Then I sock away as much as I can for another six to eight years and I'm still young enough to pop out a couple of babies. Then, if I can find a man who's smart and funny and straight and can afford to keep me in the manner to which I have become accustomed, I'll become Mrs. Whatever and live happily ever after. Yeah. Thank you…Well, we'll see…I'm also thinking I could have my eggs frozen… Yeah…Yeah. See you soon…Sure, she's right here. Bye.

(**KATIE** *holds the phone out to* **LUCY**. **LUCY** *motions that she doesn't want to take the phone.*)

JEREMY. She knows you're here.

(**LUCY** *accepts the inevitable and takes the phone.*)

(**KATIE** *exits.*)

LUCY. *(into phone)* Hello?…Hi, Mom. I can't really talk right now. How're you doing?..No kidding. That's great. You're keeping busy. Mom, I really can't talk right now…Oh, yeah. You know me. Working hard…Yes. I'm on a case right now…Well, you know, it's complicated. Lots of legal issues…No. No, I'm sure you could understand it. It's just…No. It's just I have to get going. I can't really go into it right now…Mom…Mom…

(getting upset)

Mom, I'm working really hard and I'm really surprised at you.

(crying)

You're not here to take care of me. You have to be out doing whatever it is you're doing. And if everybody else in the world comes before your own family –

(She stops crying and is instantly calm.)

She hung up.

(**LUCY** *hangs up the phone.*)

JEREMY. That is so rude.

(**JEREMY** *puts the skillet into the broiler and sets the oven timer.*)

LUCY. What am I going to do? Tell her about the case I'm working on? How do I tell her I'm defending my client's right to pump tons of mercury into the air while she's in Libya planting trees with Wangari Maathai?

JEREMY. Oh! You know who died?

LUCY. Who?

JEREMY. Gaylord Nelson.

LUCY. Who?

JEREMY. It was in the paper yesterday. I think I still have it in the recycling. Your mother's coming in for the memorial service.

(*He goes to his recycling bin and pulls out a newspaper.*)

(*reads*) "Gaylord Nelson, the folksy Democratic senator from Wisconsin who helped start the modern environmental movement with the creation of Earth Day thirty-five years ago, died Sunday. He was eighty-nine."

LUCY. Eighty-nine. That's pretty old.

JEREMY. Yeah.

LUCY. Well, now that he's dead he can start turning over in his grave.

JEREMY. There are still people who care about the environment.

LUCY. Who? Dick Cheney?

JEREMY. Hey. I'm a tree hugger. I buy blue bags. I don't run the water when I shave. I bought Bobby Kennedy Junior's book.

LUCY. Have you read it?

JEREMY. Well…There is a limit.

(**KATIE** *enters, carrying papers.*)

KATIE. I found it online. The actual term for it is septo-plasty.

JEREMY. Katie…

KATIE. It's not fair.

LUCY. I know you don't think it's fair.

KATIE. I just want to see what it would look like.

JEREMY. They have a computer so you can see what it would look like.

LUCY. *(to KATIE)* You look fine.

KATIE. I look fine? Maybe I could look better than fine.

LUCY. That's not what I meant.

KATIE. *(impersonating someone)* "Hey, there's Katie. How does she look? Oh, she looks fine."

LUCY. Katie. You're beautiful just the way you are.

KATIE. I know. I know. We're "all natural." Feminists don't get nose jobs.

LUCY. *(getting upset)* You know, you throw these terms around –

KATIE. You care about how you look.

LUCY. You think feminists eat granola and never shave.

KATIE. You get manicures.

LUCY. That's not surgery.

KATIE. Barbara Silver got a boob job for her Sweet Sixteen.

LUCY. So?!

JEREMY. *(interceding)* Right. We're not talking about that.

   (to KATIE)

   We'll talk about it later.

KATIE. *(holding the papers)* Can I just show this to her?

JEREMY. We'll talk. About. It later.

   (KATIE heads off.)

KATIE. *(as she goes)* I'll just wear a bag over my head.

   (KATIE exits.)

LUCY. She is not getting a nose job.

JEREMY. We're just…exploring the options.

LUCY. Don't give me that "deviated septum."

JEREMY. She might have a deviated septum.

(giving in)

And, yes, she wants a nose job. I thought, maybe, for her birthday.

LUCY. You're thinking about surgery for our daughter without consulting me?

JEREMY. I wasn't going to not consult you. She was telling me she didn't care about a Sweet Sixteen party and this other idea came up –

LUCY. So in lieu of a party at a restaurant, we're going to the hospital to have some plastic surgery?

JEREMY. No.

LUCY. My Sweet Sixteen was a teach-in about the objectification of women.

JEREMY. I know.

LUCY. We made a statement.

JEREMY. Well, not everything has to make a statement.

LUCY. If my daughter gets a nose job, that makes a statement.

JEREMY. I haven't said yes. Katie and I…we're just gathering information.

LUCY. And it's okay to keep Mom out of the loop on this one.

JEREMY. No. I don't want you out of the loop.

LUCY. It's just so much easier around here for you if I'm out of the loop.

JEREMY. I don't want you out of the loop. I want you in the loop. The loop is here. It's always here. I'm in the loop. Katie's in the loop. If you're not in the loop, it's because you're not here.

LUCY. I'm here now. Can we talk about it now?

JEREMY. Yes. Can you be here now?

LUCY. Yes.

JEREMY. Dr. Handler gave me the name of an ear, nose and throat guy.

LUCY. She is not getting a nose job.

JEREMY. Fine.

(beat)

We'll just keep this one last appointment.

LUCY. Jeremy…

JEREMY. We're not talking about anything drastic. It's a self-esteem issue.

LUCY. Katie does not have any problems with self-esteem.

JEREMY. I don't mean self-esteem. I mean…she's thinking about how she looks. She has a new boyfriend.

LUCY. Who? The senior?

JEREMY. No. That was over ages ago. She has a new, new boyfriend. A swimmer. Big, hunky guy. Shaves his head so there's less resistance in the water.

LUCY. That's, what, the third boyfriend this year?

JEREMY. That's right. See? You're in the loop about boyfriends. I talked to her about it. She said, "Dad. Chill. I'm no Serena Van Der Woodsen."

LUCY. Who?

*(The oven timer buzzes. **JEREMY** takes the skillet out of the broiler, transfers the frittata to a plate.)*

JEREMY. Exactly. We're both out of the loop on that one. I had to look it up on the Internet. She's a character in a book they're all reading. Like a Joan Collins, Junior.

LUCY. *(ironically)* Great.

*(**JEREMY** places the plate in front of **LUCY**.)*

JEREMY. Here you go. Bon appetit.

*(But at that moment, **LUCY**'s email arrives.)*

INTERNET VOICE (V.O.) You've got mail!

LUCY. Finally.

(She gives her attention to the computer and opens the

email. Her cell phone rings. She answers it. **JEREMY**
stands and watches her.)

LUCY. *(continuing; into phone)* Lucy Grant...Yes...I got it...
You know which passage needs to be highlighted?...

JEREMY. *(whispering, referring to the frittata)* Do you want me
to keep it warm?

*(**LUCY** shakes her head "No.")*

LUCY. *(into phone)* I want hard copies for everyone at the
table.

JEREMY. I could just –

*(**LUCY** holds up her hand to stop his talking.)*

LUCY. *(into phone)* Yes, that's the idea. I use their expert's
own report in my cross. I want lots of paper there. Got
it?...See you. 'Bye.

(She hangs up the phone.)

JEREMY. I'll just put it back in the oven.

LUCY. No. This is fine.

JEREMY. It's going to be cold.

LUCY. No. It's fine.

*(**LUCY** picks up the salt shaker and shakes salt on the
frittata.)*

LUCY. *(continuing)* This looks great. Thank you.

JEREMY. Oh, God. Please don't do that.

LUCY. What?

JEREMY. Don't put salt.

LUCY. I like salt.

JEREMY. I know you like salt. I already put salt.

LUCY. I know. I don't think you put enough salt on my
eggs.

JEREMY. I've been putting salt on your eggs for eighteen
years. I know how much salt to put on your eggs.

LUCY. I'd like to have a little extra salt this morning. Is that
all right with you?

JEREMY. You didn't even taste it. Can you taste it first and see if it needs more salt?

LUCY. I just added a little bit.

JEREMY. You put, like, a ton of salt on it.

LUCY. It's fine.

JEREMY. There's too much salt. You're not going to be able to eat it.

LUCY. I'm eating it.

(She takes a taste and has trouble swallowing it.)

LUCY. (continuing) Ack!

(quickly recovering)

They're fine.

JEREMY. I'll make you another one.

LUCY. I can eat this.

JEREMY. You can't eat this. You eat too much salt as it is. The amount of sodium you intake, one of these days, you're going to go into shock.

LUCY. You go into shock if you don't get enough sodium.

JEREMY. Well, whatever is the opposite of shock. You're going to get that.

LUCY. This is fine.

JEREMY. You can't eat this frittata! You've ruined the frittata!

(He takes the plate, walks over to the trash can, and scrapes the frittata into the trash.)

LUCY. Don't do that.

JEREMY. I'll make you another one. It'll take me a minute.

LUCY. I've got to go soon.

JEREMY. I know. I know. I'll make it quick.

LUCY. I'm starving.

JEREMY. Five minutes.

(From the top, he starts to make another frittata. As he prepares the food, he starts to sing the song he played earlier.)

JEREMY. *(sings)*

> BABY, NOW THAT I'VE FOUND YOU, I CAN'T LET YOU GO.
>
> I'LL BUILD MY WORLD AROUND YOU.

LUCY. What?

JEREMY. *(sings)*

> BABY, NOW THAT I'VE FOUND YOU, I CAN'T LET YOU GO.
>
> I'LL BUILD MY WORLD AROUND YOU.

LUCY. What are you singing?

JEREMY. *(sings, with over-articulation)*

> BABY, NOW THAT I'VE FOUND YOU, I CAN'T LET YOU GO.
>
> *(with sign language)*
>
> I'LL BUILD MY WORLD AROUND YOU.

LUCY. That's not right.

JEREMY. Yes, it is.

LUCY. No, it isn't.

JEREMY. Yes, it is.

LUCY. No, it isn't. It's not "Now that I've found you I can't let you go." It's "Now that I've found you I can let you go."

JEREMY. No, it isn't.

LUCY. Yes, it is.

JEREMY. No, it isn't. It's "Now that I've found you, I can't let you go."

LUCY. It couldn't be. It's "Now that I've found you, I *can* let you go."

JEREMY. Why would I let you go? I just found you.

LUCY. If you really love someone, you have to be willing to let them go.

JEREMY. I understand. But that's not what the song says.

LUCY. And that's okay with you.

JEREMY. I love that song. It's a great old song. It was a big hit when I was in high school.

(sings)

BABY, NOW THAT I'VE FOUND YOU –

LUCY. So now that you've found me, I'm what? I'm your prisoner?

JEREMY. No.

LUCY. I can't leave without your permission?

JEREMY. No. "Baby, now that I've found you, I can't let you go," means "I love you." I've been with other women, but now that I've found you, I'm saying I'm not going to let you go like I did those other women. I can't let you go. I want us to be together forever.

LUCY. So if you find a woman you want to be with, she has to understand that entering into a relationship with you is tantamount to giving up her freedom.

JEREMY. If I find a woman I want to be with, I'm willing to give up my freedom.

LUCY. On your terms. If this woman does choose to get into a relationship with you – And by the way, she's made it clear "she doesn't need you" –

JEREMY. *(quickly reviewing, he sings)*
YOU DON'T NEED ME, YOU DON'T NEED ME.
Granted.

LUCY. But you're the big, strong man, so even if she wants to go, you're not going to let her.

JEREMY. That's not…It's not that I'm not going to let her. It's "I can't let you go." Not "I won't let you go." You want to go? Go. Jeez.

LUCY. I don't want to go. I just want to know that if I did choose to go, I have the freedom to decide my own fate.

JEREMY. You have the freedom to decide your own fate. When have I ever said you don't have the freedom to decide your own fate? "Baby, now that I've found you, I can't let you go" means now that I've found you, I have you – And when I say I have you, I don't mean to be overly possessive – But now that I have you in my life, I can't imagine being without you.

LUCY. So if I want to go, I can go.

JEREMY. Of course, you can go. I wouldn't be happy about it. Particularly since "I've built my world around you." But if you wanted to go, I know, realistically, I couldn't stop you from going.

LUCY. So if you're in love with someone, you're still able to acknowledge the other person's freedom.

JEREMY. Certainly.

LUCY. So the song should be, "Baby, now that I've found you, I can let you go."

JEREMY. *(trying it out)*
BABY, NOW THAT I'VE FOUND YOU, I CAN LET YOU GO.
That makes no sense.

LUCY. It certainly implies a more healthy relationship.

JEREMY. It's a rock song! It's not Dr. Phil. It's making a statement. Now that I've found you, I love you so much, I can't bear the thought of you ever leaving me. I fully understand, in the back of my mind, you might leave me, but, if you do, I can still say, "I can't let you go," because even if you do leave me – Even if we're no longer in each other's presence – I found you. I have feelings of love for you in my heart. And I won't ever let go of that.

LUCY. Well, that's stupid. I think you should just move on.

JEREMY. I'm sorry you think I'm stupid.

LUCY. I don't think you're stupid.

JEREMY. Fine. "Baby, now that I've found you, I can let you go." Is that better?

LUCY. Don't you think so?

JEREMY. It's a little over-intellectual, don't you think?

LUCY. You think a relationship based on mutual respect and understanding is over-intellectual?

JEREMY. No. Not at all. But I think it means we're going to have to re-write a lot of love songs.

(sings)

ALL YOU NEED IS MUTUAL RESPECT AND
UNDERSTANDING
WA-WA-WA-WA-WA.

LUCY. All right.

JEREMY. *(sings)*

HOW SWEET IT IS TO BE MUTUALLY RESPECTED AND
UNDERSTOOD BY YOU.

LUCY. All right.

JEREMY. *(sings)*

WHAT THE WORLD NEEDS NOW
IS MUTUAL RESPECT AND UNDERSTANDING.

LUCY. All right! I'm sorry! I ruined your song. I ruined your frittata. I'm sorry. Get off my back.

JEREMY. I'll get off your back. You don't want me on your back? I'll get off your back.

(half to himself)

You don't want me on your back. You don't want me on your front. I'll just leave you alone completely.

(to **LUCY***)*

Why don't you go to McDonald's for breakfast?

LUCY. Excuse me? I don't want you on my front? When have I ever said I don't want you on my front?

JEREMY. You haven't lately.

LUCY. It hasn't been that long.

JEREMY. You don't remember the last time we –

LUCY. Yes, I do.

JEREMY. When was it?

LUCY. It hasn't been that long.

JEREMY. I can tell you exactly when the last time was.

LUCY. Okay. When?

JEREMY. I'll check my book.

LUCY. I'm in the middle of a trial.

JEREMY. I know that.

LUCY. I don't think we should have this conversation.

JEREMY. You don't think we should have any conversation. Unless it's some intellectual discourse –

LUCY. I'm in the middle of a trial.

JEREMY. And I'm on the outskirts! Out here! Clinging to my ever decreasing status in our relationship.

LUCY. Well, I'm sorry, I don't have time to feel sorry for you right now. I have enough male ego to deal with at work.

JEREMY. Yeah, cause we're all just a bunch of jerks, aren't we?

LUCY. You said it.

JEREMY. Great. I'm a man so that automatically makes me a jerk, right?

LUCY. You're the exception. You're mother didn't raise you to be a jerk. She raised you to be a sensitive guy.

JEREMY. You know what? Don't give my mother all the credit. Just because I was a nice Jewish boy doesn't mean I couldn't be an asshole.

LUCY. Fine.

JEREMY. I used to treat women like sex objects. Remember the Sexual Revolution? The minute I heard about the Sexual Revolution, I went out to enlist. Everybody thought it was about "peace" and "love," but I knew what it was really about. It was an excuse to get a lot of sex, no questions asked.

LUCY. I know.

JEREMY. Then 1972, I'm at I.S.U. I see Marlo Thomas campaigning for Shirley Chisholm for president and I had such hots for Marlo Thomas...But who got Marlo Thomas?

LUCY. Phil Donahue.

JEREMY. Phil Donahue. There was Phil Donahue. And Alan Alda. And I saw it was good to be a nice guy. And it wasn't easy. I went back and forth. "I'm a nice guy. I'm an asshole. I'm a nice guy. I'm an asshole." Like Faye Dunaway in "Chinatown." "She's my sister. She's my daughter. She's my sister. She's my daughter." So I went to sensitivity training and encounter groups. I read Betty Friedan and Germaine Greer and Carol Gilligan. I raised my own damn consciousness. And then 1979.

LUCY. "Kramer vs. Kramer."

JEREMY. "Kramer vs. Kramer." I saw "Kramer vs. Kramer" fourteen times. Like it was a training film. And I got it. Men can be the nurturers. We can get off the fast track. So I quit my job at Leo Burnett and wrote my first novel about – Hey! – An asshole who becomes a sensitive guy. I was right there along with Mr. Mom and Mrs. Doubtfire and Three Men and a Baby. And I thought, "Great. This is it. This is the way it's going to be. You bring home the bacon and I'll make the quiche."

LUCY. I know this.

JEREMY. I know you know this. So don't say, "all men are jerks." It pisses me off. I achieved "sensitive guy-dom" through hard work and determination. I am a husband and father totally different from the way my father was a husband and father. And what do I get for it? You'll find me in the Museum of Pop Culture. Next to pet rocks and leisure suits.

(KATIE enters.)

JEREMY. *(to KATIE)* What?!

KATIE. Nothing.

(KATIE exits.)

JEREMY. *(stopping her)* What? No. Wait. Katie. It's all right. Come on.

(KATIE enters.)

You ready to go?

KATIE. Yeah. I just have to finish one paper.

JEREMY. What on?

KATIE. "The Road Not Taken" by Robert Frost.

JEREMY. Oh, that's a great poem.

KATIE. It's okay.

JEREMY. What are you writing about?

KATIE. You know. The imagery. The setting.

JEREMY. What about it?

KATIE. Well, you know. Two roads. Two possibilities. Two choices. Make up your mind, Dude.

JEREMY. Well, it's not that simple.

KATIE. I know. I know. Two roads diverged in a yellow wood and I have to choose which path to take and I stand there for a really long time and, finally, I take the road less traveled by.

JEREMY. And that has made all the difference.

KATIE. Right. I got it.

JEREMY. So you think that's a good thing? To take the road less traveled by?

KATIE. Sure.

JEREMY. It may not be easy. It may require fortitude and perseverance. And I doubt that you should ever come back.

KATIE. I know.

JEREMY. But if you take the road less traveled by, that can make all the difference.

KATIE. Dad. I got it.

JEREMY. Okay.

(LUCY *adds her own quiet reflection.*)

LUCY. I don't know why everybody thinks that poem is so fucking optimistic.

(KATIE *and* JEREMY *look at* LUCY.)

What's so great about taking the road less traveled by? So it makes all the difference. What if the difference it makes turns out to be crummy?

JEREMY. Well, I don't think that's what Frost is saying.

LUCY. Where does it say he's so thrilled about making all the difference?

(quoting)

"I shall be telling this with a sigh." You don't sigh when you're happy. You sigh when you realize nothing turned out the way you thought it was going to.

JEREMY. I don't think a sigh necessarily means he's unhappy. He says,

(quoting)

"I shall be telling this with a sigh/ Somewhere ages and ages hence/ Two roads diverged in a wood, and I."

(explaining)

Sigh rhymes with I.

LUCY. Sigh is the only word that rhymes with I? Why didn't he write, "I shall be telling this…by and by?" Or, "I shall be telling this…gettin' high?" He's sighing. He's made his choice and he's stuck with it.

*(**LUCY** exhales and it is one long, plaintive sigh.)*

(Silence.)

JEREMY. *(to **KATIE**, quietly)* Go finish your paper.

KATIE. I can't. I'm too depressed.

*(**KATIE** exits. Silence.)*

JEREMY. We have to talk.

LUCY. What?

JEREMY. I can't take this anymore. I'm trying to keep things together around here and you're sucking up all the positive energy in the joint.

LUCY. Well, why don't I hire someone to do the cooking and the cleaning and I won't have to listen to all the judgments.

JEREMY. Excuse me. Who's making judgments, counselor?

LUCY. I'm not telling you you're "sucking up all the positive energy." I'm out there busting my butt so that you can stay home and read poetry and run 10K's and make frittatas.

JEREMY. I'm running this household so that you –

LUCY. You're running this household?

JEREMY. Yes.

LUCY. *(sarcastically)* You're doing such a great job.

JEREMY. You wouldn't have a clue.

> (**LUCY** *points to the boarded up window.*)

LUCY. Why don't you ever fix that window?
> (**JEREMY** *looks at the window and then back at* **LUCY.**)

JEREMY. What's wrong with it?

LUCY. *(as if she has to state the obvious)* It's broken?

JEREMY. I thought you liked it like that. Like it's some memorial to your father. All it needs is a plaque. "Window broken by Stewart Grant. Circa 1970."

LUCY. Every time I look at it, it reminds me of when we walked out on him. How guilty I felt.

JEREMY. Your mom never felt any guilt.

LUCY. So I had to feel guilty enough for the both of us. *Some*body had to feel guilty, don't you think? The way he got shafted?

JEREMY. That was a long time ago.

LUCY. So? Does guilt fade away with time? Or does it accrue interest like money in a bank?

JEREMY. We're living here fifteen years, that's the first time you've ever mentioned that window.

LUCY. It is not.

JEREMY. I'll check my book.

LUCY. Stop saying you'll check your book.

JEREMY. You used to think that was charming.

LUCY. I used to think a lot of things were charming. Now I just find them really annoying.

JEREMY. Well, if you're so annoyed, why don't you just go to work.

LUCY. Maybe you'd like me to spend more hours at the office.

JEREMY. Whatever makes you happy.

LUCY. You don't think I'd like to see Katie play soccer this weekend? You get to see every game ever. You got to see everything and I have to watch it on video.

JEREMY. And that's my fault? You made your choice.

LUCY. You made your choice.

JEREMY. So maybe we made the wrong choices.

LUCY. Maybe we did.

JEREMY. Maybe we should just go back to the way it was.

LUCY. You'd like to go back to the way it was.

JEREMY. When roles were clearly defined? When every little thing didn't have to be negotiated? Sometimes, I think –

LUCY. You'd like to be the way my father was.

JEREMY. I could be like him if I wanted to be. The way your father used to give your mother the "silent treatment?"

(JEREMY *sits down at the table opposite* LUCY, *glares at her, and doesn't say a word for about five seconds. He gets up.*)

JEREMY. All right, I don't have that kind of discipline. You father was in the military. He must have learned it there. Anyway, that's not what I want.

LUCY. What do you want?

JEREMY. I can't even tell you.

LUCY. What do you want?

JEREMY. I want to be Rob Petrie! All right? I want to have a job. I want to go to work and be in a roomful of fun Jews and have loads of laughs. And then I want to come home to my happy child and my loving wife. And I'll come in and maybe I'll trip over the ottoman and maybe I won't, but that's up to me because I'm the man of the house. And then we'll have dinner and, then after dinner, we'll have the gang over and tell jokes and do a couple of numbers and have loads of laughs. And sometimes, there'll be a little misunderstanding and we won't know what's wrong except then

I'll fix it and we'll work it out and my wife will go, "Oh, Rob!" and everything will be right with the world and everyone will be happy.

(pause)

I'm sorry. That was so incredibly retro...

LUCY. I had no idea you were so unhappy.

JEREMY. I'm not unhappy. It's just that, lately, I've been feeling...kind of...unhappy. What's the point anymore? Half of all marriages end in divorce. Why fight it? You're exhausted. I'm exhausted. Why don't we just split up?

LUCY. I don't know. Why don't we?

JEREMY. I don't know. Okay. Fine. Then, what? I guess you'll move out.

LUCY. *I'll* move out? Excuse me. I think you'll move out.

JEREMY. Why should I move out? You're hardly ever here.

LUCY. This is my house. I was born in this house. It was my idea for us to move in here after my father died.

JEREMY. So, what? You think you're going to live here forever?

LUCY. Until they carry me out on a stretcher. If this piece of real estate is the only thing in my life that is real, then so be it. I want *something* in my life that's permanent.

JEREMY. Well, I don't want to move out. I love this house.

LUCY. Then why don't you fix the window?!

JEREMY. All right! Fine! I'll fix the window!

(He goes to a cabinet and pulls out a drawer. But he pulls too hard and the drawer comes all the way out of the cabinet and spills its contents onto the floor.)

JEREMY. Crap!

(He scoops up two handfuls of stuff, drops them in the drawer, and tries to slide the drawer back into the cabinet. As he tries to line up the drawer, he peers into the cabinet and notices something in there.)

JEREMY. What is that?

(He reaches in and pulls out a book.)

JEREMY. This is *The Feminine Mystique.*

LUCY. *(incredulous)* What?

JEREMY. Is this yours?

LUCY. No.

> *(JEREMY opens the front cover and looks at the facing page. He smiles.)*

JEREMY. This was your mother's.

LUCY. How can you tell?

JEREMY. Look.

> *(He shows the book to her.)*

She wrote in her name. "Mrs. Stewart Grant." And then she crossed it out and wrote, "Susan Grant."

LUCY. Wow.

> *(JEREMY leafs through the book. A passage catches his eye and he reads it.)*
>
> *(reading)*

"Who knows of the possibilities of love when men and women share not only children, home, and garden, not only the fulfillment of their biological roles, but the responsibilities and passions of the work that creates the human future and the full human knowledge of who they are." Oh.

LUCY. That was the idea, wasn't it?

JEREMY. *(referring to the book)* To share...

LUCY. To share.

JEREMY. The responsibilities and passions of the work that creates the human future.

LUCY. We're supposed to be working together. Not just... Coexisting.

JEREMY. For the sake of the future.

LUCY. For the sake of the future of the young woman upstairs.

JEREMY. We could do that. Then if we could just get

universal health care and federally funded day care and fully flexible work scheduling...Then you'd have real family values in this country.

LUCY. Then we'd be Finland.

JEREMY. It'll happen.

LUCY. No. It's like we're going backwards. Promise Keepers. Dr. Laura. Women will never get paid the same as men. I'll never get the corner office.

JEREMY. Yes, you will.

LUCY. No. I got passed over again.

JEREMY. *(stunned)* What?

LUCY. Yesterday. Howard is retiring.

JEREMY. He is?

LUCY. He told me I'm such a highly valued member of the firm. But he's giving his client list to Danny Stephens.

JEREMY. Oh, no.

LUCY. They play golf together. Danny Stephens is going to get a bigger office than me because he can hit a little ball with a stick.

JEREMY. That's not right.

LUCY. Then I hear that Danny is having his celebration at some Japanese place downtown. So I'm a team player, right? After work, I stop in to congratulate him and he's in there with a bunch of guys eating sushi off the body of a naked woman.

JEREMY. Omigod. *(sympathetic)* I'm sorry, Honey. What do you want to do?

LUCY. I don't know. If it isn't happening now, it's never going to happen.

JEREMY. Maybe it will.

LUCY. No. I should quit. But then what would I do?

JEREMY. You could hang out your own shingle.

LUCY. Oy.

JEREMY. Well, whatever you want to do. We're partners. I'm on your side. When times get rough.

(*He begins to sing "Bridge Over Troubled Water."*)

AND FRIENDS JUST CAN'T BE FOUND.

(**LUCY** *smiles.*)

LIKE A BRIDGE OVER TROUBLED WATER
I WILL LAY ME DOWN

LUCY. You can still make me smile.

JEREMY. Then there's hope.

(*The oven timer buzzes.* **JEREMY** *removes the skillet from the broiler, transfers the frittata to a plate, and places it in front of* **LUCY**.)

JEREMY. Here.

LUCY. Thank you.

JEREMY. Would you please taste it to see if it needs salt?

(*She takes a taste.*)

LUCY. That's delicious.

JEREMY. Thank you.

LUCY. You didn't have to bother.

JEREMY. I always make a special breakfast on our anniversary.

(**LUCY** *stops. She's mortified. She hangs her head in shame.*)

LUCY. I'm such a loser.

JEREMY. No you're not.

LUCY. You should leave me.

JEREMY. I'm not going to leave you.

LUCY. I'm so tired.

JEREMY. I know.

LUCY. I hope you don't leave me.

JEREMY. I'm not going to leave you.

LUCY. I'm so sorry. I can't believe…I forgot our anniversary.

(*imitating Laura Petrie*)

Oh, Rob!

JEREMY. You know what else? When you're done with your trial, why don't we let Katie have some quality time with my parents and you and I go find a quiet beach somewhere in a tropical climate?

LUCY. That would be nice.

JEREMY. And I'll tell you about my new novel. I'm going to try something really risky. It's a story in which the men and women aren't miserable. It's about a happy family.

LUCY. *(quoting)* "Happy families are all alike."

JEREMY. You know…that fuckin' Leo Tolstoy. I hate that. That one line has single-handedly done more damage to more artists trying to send a positive message. On top of which, you know what I think? I think he's wrong. He got it wrong. I think Unhappy families are all alike. I've seen them over and over again. On Jerry Springer and Dr. Phil and "Desperate Housewives." Everybody's Unhappy. Everybody's dysfunctional. All the children are abused. All the husbands wish their wives were younger. All the wives wish their husbands dicks would fall off.

LUCY. I don't wish your dick would fall off.

JEREMY. I can't tell you how much that means to me. Why does everything have to be all about conflict and pain and perversion? Why can't something be worthwhile that's uplifting and hopeful?

LUCY. I don't know.

JEREMY. Because that's not the way the world is. The world really is horrible and miserable. So those of us that still believe in the possibility of happy endings are the ones who have to keep on fighting. Your mother's been out there for thirty-five years and she still believes she can save the earth. Better to plant one tree than to curse global warming. Better to light one candle than to curse the darkness, right? Are you with me?

LUCY. We're partners.

JEREMY. Then let's be the candle in the darkness.

(He points to the boarded up window.)

Let's let in the light.

(He goes to the window.)

I will fix this window for you, my dear.

(He goes to the window and grabs hold of the board to pull it down but it won't budge. LUCY gets up and goes over to help.)

Let's…Let's…

(It still won't budge. LUCY looks around at the stuff that fell out of the drawer. She spies a hammer, picks it up, and hands it to JEREMY.)

LUCY. Try this.

JEREMY. Thank you.

(He jams the claw end of the hammer underneath the board and pulls on it with all of his might. It creaks and loosens a bit. He moves the hammer to another spot.)

(grunting)

Let's let in the light!

(While he's working on the window, KATIE enters.)

KATIE. Dad, can you take me?

(KATIE sees what JEREMY is doing. She turns to Lucy.)

KATIE. *(grossed out)* Mom! Dad's trying to be handy!

(JEREMY loosens the board and it falls away. The window with the hole in it is seen in all its glory. Sunlight streams into the room. Perhaps some beatific music is heard. JEREMY turns to LUCY. She gets up and goes to stand by his side. KATIE joins them. They stand in the glow for a moment. Then the clouds move in. Thunder is heard. And it starts to rain. The family stands together and watches it.)

FADE OUT

END OF PLAY

PROPERTIES

Act One

Juice squeezer
Cutting board
Coffee cups
Newspaper
Oranges
Strainer
Loaf of bread
Bowl with chicken salad
Trash can
Dishtowels
Juice glasses
Plastic sandwich bags
Paper lunch bags
Covered casserole dish
Refrigerator magnets
Gas mask
Coffee pot
Telephone
Frying pan
Eggs
Cereal
Cereal bowl
Bottle of milk
Spoon
Plates
Spatula
Pen
Notebook
Book including Robert Frost poems
Copy of *The Feminine Mystique* by Betty Friedan

<u>*Act Two*</u>
Microwave oven
Cordless phone
Electric juicer
Newspaper
Law books
Laptop computer
Legal pads
Oranges
Sharp knife
Cutting board
Juice glasses
Cell phones
Coffee mugs
Coffee pot with coffee maker
CD
Boombox
Milk
Eggs
Zucchini
Red peppers
Colander/strainer
Carton of Yogurt
Spoon
Non-stick skillet
Recycling bin
Plates
Forks
Knives
Salt shaker
Trash can
Computer papers
Miscellaneous "junk drawer" items
Copy of *The Feminine Mystique* by Betty Friedan
Hammer

COSTUME PLOT

Act One

SUSAN
Rust dress and vest, red shoes, rust floral print apron, gold wedding band

STEWART
Blue polyester shirt, blue/yellow striped tie, brown pants, brown belt w/gold buckle, burgundy slip-on shoes, watch with brown strap, gold wedding band, eyeglasses

LUCY
Peach/pink striped pajamas, peach quilted robe, pink terry cloth slippers, white socks, white/yellow floral print top, brown suede fringed vest, brown corduroy skirt, cream knee-high socks, brown leather loafers, white macrame bag

Act Two

LUCY
Grey suit jacket, grey suit pants, blue silk blouse, sling back shoes, silver watch, silver faux diamond earrings, reading glasses, silver/diamond wedding band

JEREMY
Grey t-shirt, green plaid shirt, light khaki pants, brown belt w/silver buckle, silver wedding band

KATIE
Grey hoodie sweatshirt, green Paul Frank t-shirt, green Paul Frank pajama pants, pink zip up shirt with flowers, blue ripped jeans, grey camisole, brown belt, gold hoop dangly earrings, blue messenger bag, white sneakers

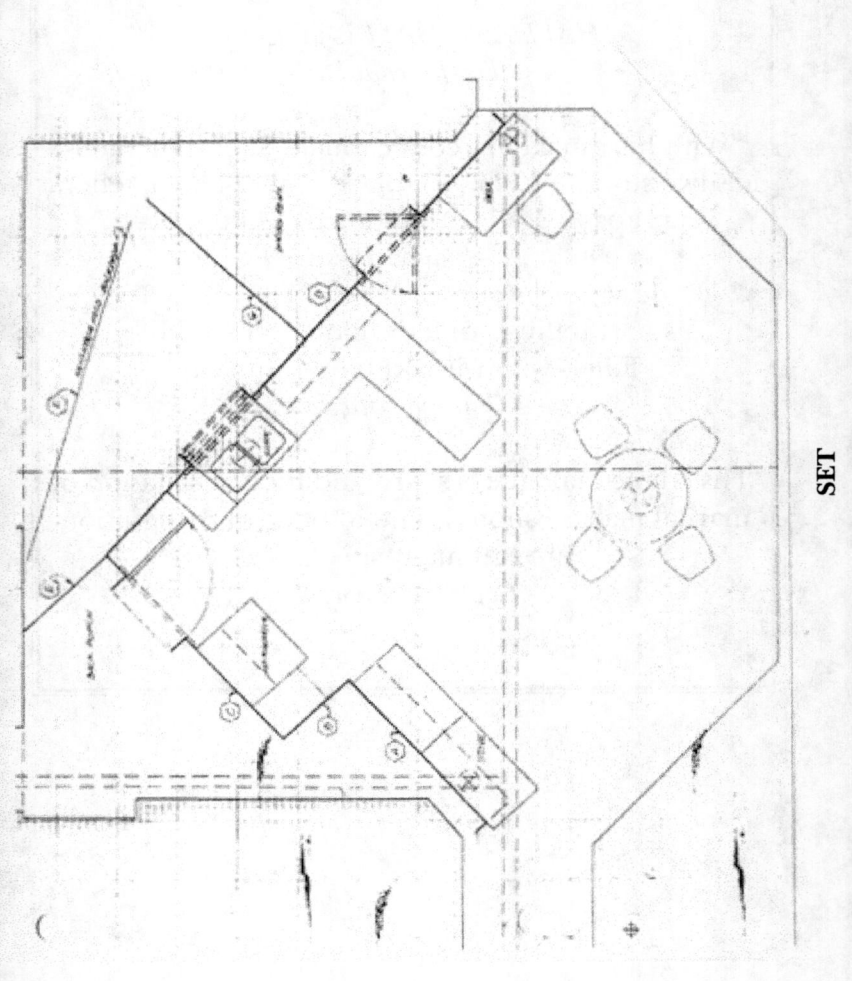

SET

Also by
JAMES SHERMAN...

Affluenza!

Beau Jest

From Door to Door

The God of Isaac

Magic Time

OTHER TITLES AVAILABLE FROM SAMUEL FRENCH

DEAD CITY
Sheila Callaghan

Full Length / Comic Drama / 3m, 4f / Unit Set

It's June 16, 2004. Samantha Blossom, a chipper woman in her 40s, wakes up one June morning in her Upper East Side apartment to find her life being narrated over the airwaves of public radio. She discovers in the mail an envelope addressed to her husband from his lover, which spins her raw and untethered into an odyssey through the city… a day full of chance encounters, coincidences, a quick love affair, and a fixation on the mysterious Jewel Jupiter. Jewel, the young but damaged poet genius, eventually takes a shine to Samantha and brings her on a midnight tour of the meat-packing district which changes Samantha's life forever—or doesn't. This 90 minute comic drama is a modernized, gender-reversed, relocated, hyper-theatrical riff on the novel Ulysses, occurring exactly 100 years to the day after Joyce's jaunt through Dublin.

"Wonderful... Sheila Callaghan's pleasingly witty and theatrical new drama that is a love letter to New York masquerading as hate mail... [Callaghan] writes with a world-weary tone and has a poet's gift for economical description.
The entire dead city comes alive..."
- New York Times

"*Dead City,* Sheila Callaghan's riff on James Joyce's Ulysses is stylish, lyrical, fascinating, occasionally irritating, and eminently worthwhile... the kind of work that is thoroughly invigorating."
- Backstage

SAMUELFRENCH.COM

OTHER TITLES AVAILABLE FROM SAMUEL FRENCH

JACK GOES BOATING
Bob Glaudini

Full Length / Comedy / 2m, 2f / Interior
Four flawed but likeable lower-middle-class New Yorkers interact in a touching and warmhearted play about learning how to stay afloat in the deep water of day-to-day living. Laced with cooking classes, swimming lessons and a smorgasbord of illegal drugs, *Jack Goes Boating* is a story of date panic, marital meltdown, betrayal, and the prevailing grace of the human spirit.

"An immensely likable play [that] exudes a wry compassion."
- *The New York Times*

"Endearing romantic comedy about a married couple and the social-misfit friends they fix up. Witty and knowing and all heart."
- *Variety*

"Glides effortlessly from the shallow end of the emotional pool to the deep end."
- *Theatremania.com*

www.ingramcontent.com/pod-product-compliance
Lightning Source LLC
Chambersburg PA
CBHW070646120726
47909CB00004B/1599